GEO

5.16

Lexile: _____

AR/BL: _____

AR Points: _____

Earth Matters
Life

Dana Meachen Rau

Marshall Cavendish
Benchmark
New York

2

Earth has water. Earth is not too cold or too hot. Earth is the only place we know that has living things.

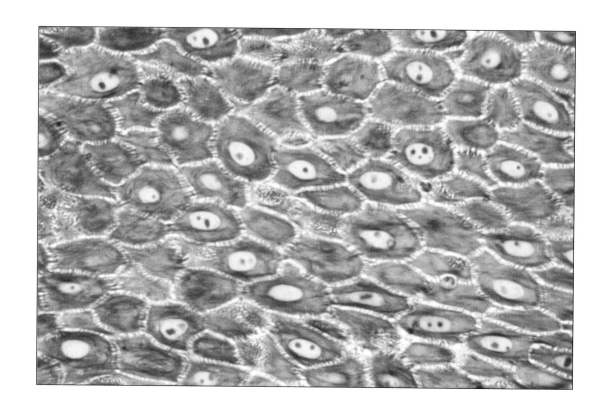

Living things are made up
of cells. *Cells* are like tiny
building blocks.

Lots of cells together build living things. You may have as many as 100 trillion cells in your body!

Animals are living things. Plants are living things. *Fungi* are living things.

Some living things have only one cell. They are so small you need a *microscope* to see them.

Living things grow and change.
Green plants can grow taller.
They can turn toward the Sun.

A kind of fungi called *mold* can grow on bread or an old piece of fruit.

Animals grow and change, too. A caterpillar turns into a butterfly.

A hare's fur changes from brown to white.

Living things *reproduce*.
They can make more of their
own kind.

A plant makes seeds. Seeds
fall to the ground and grow into
more plants.

A mushroom makes *spores* to reproduce. Wind blows spores to new places. Spores grow into new mushrooms.

Some animals lay eggs. Frogs lay eggs in water. Snakes lay eggs on land.

Birds keep their eggs safe in a nest.

Some animals have live babies.
A whale has one baby at a time.

A cat has a *litter*.

Living things need *energy*. Green plants get energy from the Sun. They use this energy to make their food.

Fungi cannot make their own food. Some fungi get energy from dead things in soil.

Animals need energy, too.
Some animals eat plants for
energy. A squirrel eats nuts.

Some animals eat other animals. A bear eats fish.

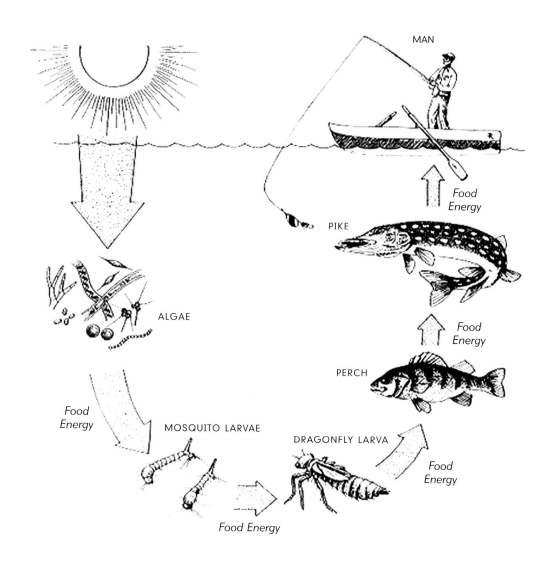

MAN

Food
Energy

PIKE

Food
Energy

ALGAE

PERCH

Food
Energy

Food
Energy

MOSQUITO LARVAE

DRAGONFLY LARVA

Food
Energy

Food Energy

Food and energy move from one living thing to another. This is called a *food chain*.

A plant gets energy from the Sun.

A mouse eats the plant. An owl eats the mouse. This is a food chain.

We share Earth with many living things. Earth gives us air to breathe. It gives us food to eat. It is good to be alive!

Challenge Words

cells (sells)—Tiny building blocks that make up living things.

energy (EN-uhr-jee)—The power to work or be active.

food chain—How food and energy move from one living thing to another.

fungi (FUN-jee)—Living things that absorb their food from dead or living things.

litter (LIT-ehr)—A group of kittens or other baby animals born at the same time.

microscope (MY-kruh-skohp)—A tool used to see things that are very small.

mold—A type of fungi.

reproduce (ree-pruh-DOOS)—To make more of something or to have babies.

spores (spors)—Tiny bodies that some fungi use to reproduce themselves.

Index

Page numbers in **boldface** are illustrations.

With thanks to Nanci Vargus, Ed.D., and Beth Walker Gambro, reading consultants

Marshall Cavendish Benchmark
99 White Plains Road
Tarrytown, New York 10591-5502
www.marshallcavendish.us

Library of Congress Cataloging-in-Publication Data

Rau, Dana Meachen, 1971–
Life / by Dana Meachen Rau.
p. cm. — (Bookworms. Earth matters)
Summary: "Discusses all the different forms of life on Earth, including plants and animals"—Provided by publisher.
Includes index.
ISBN 978-0-7614-3044-5
1. Life (Biology)—Juvenile literature. I. Title.
QH501.R38 2008
570—dc22
2007030275

Editor: Christina Gardeski
Publisher: Michelle Bisson
Designer: Virginia Pope
Art Director: Anahid Hamparian

Photo Research by Anne Burns Images

Cover Photo by *Alamy Images*/Don Smith

The photographs in this book are used with permission and through the courtesy of:
Corbis: pp. 1, 20 Jorma Jamsen/zefa; p. 2 Paul A. Souders; p. 7T John Francis Bourke/zefa; p. 13 Dale C. Spartas; p. 15 W. Wayne Lockwood; p. 18 Amos Nachoum; p. 19 DK Limited; p. 22 Yann Arthus-Bertrand; p. 26 Scott Sinklier. *Photo Researchers*: pp. 4, 9T Biophoto Associates; p. 9B AJPhoto; p. 10 Kenneth M. Highfill. *Alamy Images*: p. 5 Woody Stock; p. 8 Richard Osbourne; p. 23 David Sharp. *Peter Arnold*: p. 7B Roland Birke; p. 16 Sylvain Cordier; p. 27 W. Layer. *Animals Animals*: p. 11 Darren Bennett; p. 12 David Boyle; p. 17 Steven David Miller; p. 21 John Lemker. *Photri*: p. 24. *SuperStock*: p. 29 Blend Images.

Printed in Malaysia
1 3 5 6 4 2